WIT...
From ...
Junior Sch...
Library

where
as a
Film
h the
: ten
lren's
won
3, he
dren.

Books by the same author

Fat Boy Saves World
The Ghost of Johnny Savage
The Puppet

Winning Back DAD

IAN BONE

Illustrations by

CRAIG SMITH

WALKER BOOKS
AND SUBSIDIARIES
LONDON • BOSTON • SYDNEY

Promotion of this title has been assisted by the
South Australian Government through Arts SA.

A R T S A

First published 1999 by Walker Books Ltd
87 Vauxhall Walk, London SE11 5HJ

This edition published 2000

Walker Books' Subsidiaries:

Candlewick Press Inc.
2067 Massachusetts Avenue
Cambridge, MA 02140, USA

Walker Books Australia Pty Ltd and
Walker Books New Zealand Ltd
Level 2, 1 – 15 Wilson Street
Locked Bag 22, Newtown, NSW 2042, Australia

2 4 6 8 10 9 7 5 3

This book has been typeset in Plantin.

Printed and bound in Great Britain by
The Guernsey Press Co. Ltd

British Library Cataloguing in Publication Data
A catalogue record for this book
is available from the British Library.

ISBN 0-7445-7291-6

For Jack, Elinor, Bridget and Rose ...
who gave me so much nappy practice

Contents

Chapter One

Chapter One

The first thing I want to tell you about my dad is how he did his Trucking Tummy Trick. We'd be driving along the open road in his truck, just the two of us, when he'd suddenly call out, "Hey, Kel, my boy, watch this." Then he'd take his hands off the steering wheel and push his fat tummy out. My dad's stomach is so big and floppy that it could squeeze around the steering wheel like a hand. It's true!

Next he'd lift his bum up off the seat and sway from side to side. The whole rig would wobble down the dead-straight road. Only my dad could think of steering a truck that way.

Once when he was doing his Trick he did a fart. I laughed so much that he had to pat me on the back and say, "Settle down, boy." You try keeping a straight face when your dad does something like that!

Dad used to sing too when he was driving his truck, with a big grin on his face that made him look like a little kid up to no good. He'd sing so loud, "I'm the king of the road…" or "Going home to see my bay-beeee…" I think he meant my little sister, Bridey, when he sang about his "bay-beeee".

He was the best truck driver in the district, that's what Norman O'Brien said. But my mum said, "You don't want to be letting Norman O'Brien sweet talk you." She's funny, my mum, and she's Irish too. When she speaks she sounds like a song without any music, or a singer without a piano. Dad says she talks with an "Oirish Lep-Re-Karn accent". But whenever he says that Mum kicks him in the shin. She never misses.

I loved going on the truck with my da. He'd take me and Mum on the short runs, with a load of sheep in the trailer stinking and baa-ing. But after a while Mum got too uncomfortable because she was pregnant with Bridey, so I became Dad's "co-driver". We were a team, Dad and me. We started driving a long run, leaving Friday and returning Monday morning.

They were the best of times.

Malcolm Prentis said I'd turn into a moron because I was missing out on some school. That's the sort of comment you can expect from Malcolm.

Da laughed when I told him about it. "You ain't no moron, Kel," he said. "You're the brains of this outfit, that's for sure."

And I smiled so wide that I thought my face might crack. After that he started calling me "the ideas man". And that was true because I would sit next to him in the cab and tell him all about my ideas for truck driving and schoolwork and winning at sport. Sometimes Da would nod at my plans and say, "Now why didn't I think of that?" Then he'd grin, and I'd grin, and the highway would wobble in the hot sun. That was us, the team, driving down our highway.

Some mornings we'd stop at a café for eggs and bacon. The place would usually be filled with other truck drivers who drove the same run. "Here comes the Professor," they'd say to me.

Truck drivers love to make up nicknames. Da's nickname was Mr All Night Long because he could drive all night long with only a few rest stops if he wanted to. Dad said it was because of his *tortoise* driving method: slow and steady.

I should tell you about his red cap, too. He wore it all the time, pulled down low when he was tired or pushed back when he wasn't. It was so dirty. All around the inside of that cap there was this greasy black smudge from Dad's hair.

And it had the word KING sewn across the front in yellow stitching. That's what he was, for sure. The King of the Road.

Until the day he came home without his red cap.

Chapter Two

Chapter Two

The afternoon my dad came home without his red cap, I was peeling an orange on the front porch.

My mum calls our house a "little Aussie cottage in the middle of a thousand wheat fields". I tried counting the wheat fields once, but I got bored, so I'm not sure if there are one thousand or not. I suppose you'll have to take my mother's word for it. She says the Irish never lie.

I was listening to the sounds of the highway, which is at the end of our dusty road. I heard cars driving to Dawson, the nearest town, and trucks zooming to the city. Then I heard the one magic sound I was waiting for, and I stopped peeling the orange. It was truck gears building up from low to high, heading down our road.

I ran to the screen door and shouted, "Da's home!"

He was still going to take a while to get to our house: his truck isn't very fast. But you try telling that to my little sister, Bridey. She ran out on to the porch, her nappy all wet and sagging, looking for Dad. He'd been away on an extra-long run. Bridey walked to the fence, then back down the side of the house looking for him.

After a while she stomped up to me, "Da? Da?" and it didn't matter how many times I told her he'd be here soon, she kept on asking. So I took her down to the fence. A little dust storm blew up, and I turned my back to it, covering Bridey's eyes with my T-shirt.

Mum calls Bridey "Little Miss Extreme", because she is either extremely annoying or extremely cute. Little Miss Extreme begged me to pick her up. Picking up my baby sister without going near her nappy is one of the skills I've learnt as an older brother. I finally got her sitting on the fat fence post and she was happy.

Dad's truck was quite close now. I whispered in Bridey's ear that her da was going to give her a big hug and a kiss, like he always did. She listened hard, her hot little breath on my cheek.

When she saw the dust cloud from the truck she got excited and tried to stand up. Her legs missed the post and she toppled forward. I just caught her. Then she turned round and grabbed at my T-shirt. She was crying from the fright and her little fingers pinched me so hard that I nearly cried too. I tried to put her down but she wouldn't let go. I could feel a cold, wet patch growing on my T-shirt. Then the little terror put her arms around my head and tried to climb me like a possum up a tree. She was pulling on my hair, dragging the wet patch up my T-shirt towards my mouth when I finally heard the truck pull up at our gate.

I yelled, "Look, Da's home now. He's

here!" but she still wouldn't budge. Then I looked up myself to see what the problem was.

That's when I had the second biggest shock in my life. It wasn't my dad's truck outside our gate. It was a strange rig, painted orange and blue, with someone else's name on it.

The passenger door opened and my dad hopped down with a swag over his shoulder. He waved to the driver of the orange rig, then slammed the door shut. The driver gave a blast of the horn and moved off slowly.

"Who was that?" I asked as Dad walked past me. But he didn't answer, just shook his head. He had this awful look on his face, real tough and dark. He kept on walking towards the house and Bridey had a fit. Mum came out and grabbed her, then turned to Dad and said, "So you've done it?" and he just nodded.

"Done what, Mum?" I asked, but she was too busy with Bridey to answer, soothing her curly head and speaking in her singing voice.

I ran into the house, where I found Dad in the kitchen, staring out of the window. He turned to me and tried to smile but he wasn't very good at it.

"Sorry, mate," he said. "But we was losing money badly. I had to sell it."

"Sell what?" I asked.

"The rig, mate. I sold my truck. It's gone back to the dealer."

And that was the *biggest* shock I've ever had in my life. How could he sell our truck? Why?

I wanted to yell at Dad, but I didn't. My throat went all dry and my stomach felt like someone had kicked it. I sat down at the table and Dad got me a glass of water. He said I looked like I'd seen a ghost.

But it wasn't a ghost that was bothering me, it was him. What did he think he was doing selling the truck? How was he going to be King of the Road now?

How were we going to be a team?

Chapter Three

Chapter Three

I was so gobsmacked that it was a week later
before I realized Da didn't have his red
KING cap any more. When I asked him
about it he just shrugged, said he must have
left it in the truck. "Well, go back and get it,"
I said, but he told me it was too late now. I
couldn't believe my ears. He wouldn't say it
was too late if he'd left some money behind in
the truck. Oh no. He'd be back as quick as a
shot to get that.

Money was all he ever talked about after he
sold the truck. I'd hear him say things to
Mum like, "What am I gonna do to earn a
crust?" He rang up everyone he knew and
asked them for a job. They didn't have one.
Then he rang up everyone he didn't know,
but they didn't have any work either. He
looked worried all the time.

Then one Saturday morning Da was reading the newspaper when he suddenly screwed it up and threw it into the fireplace. "I'll never get a job," he yelled, his face going bright red. "I'm just no good for nothing." And he stomped out of the kitchen.

I felt really scared when he said that. I had to walk around the house a couple of times, kick a bull-ants' nest and tear an old branch apart before I could think straight. I was mad with him for saying he was "no good for nothing". He was the best dad around.

Mum was angry too. She told him to "Stop acting like a *babbee*." Da wouldn't listen to her, so Mum hopped into the car and drove to Dawson. It was weird, Dad sulking in the bedroom and me playing with Bridey, wondering all the time what was going on.

Then Mum came back with a big grin on her face.

Da said, "What's up?"

"I've been touched by the wings of fate," said Mum.

"How?" I asked.

"Well, I was still feeling mad with your da," she said, "and I took to walking up and down the streets like, when I saw a sign."

"I suppose it was from the angels," said Dad, sounding like he didn't believe her.

"Actually," smiled Mum, "it was from the supermarket. Taped to the window, saying they needed a new cashier."

"What's that got to do with us?" asked Da.

"I'm the new cashier, you great lump," laughed Mum. "I've got us a job."

Isn't that brilliant? Now Da didn't have to be worried about money. He kept saying, "I suppose it'll work out … for a while at least." And Mum said, "Think of all the time you'll have with the little one and Kel."

So it was done – Da stayed home and looked after little Bridey and Mum went to work.

It sounded like a good idea to me. I'd come home from school and tell Da about my ideas, just like the old days. Mum would go to work and earn money, and after a while they'd get enough to buy another truck. And in the meantime, me and Da would still keep the team together.

But it didn't happen like that. Da seemed to have new things to worry about. Running after Bridey, cleaning, cooking and hanging out nappies. And when he wasn't worrying about all that he was bossing me around. "Kel, take your sister outside for a play, will ya?" or "Kel, peel them potatoes."

He was even more grumpy. Like the time we were driving along in the car and I looked at his tummy. It barely touched the steering wheel and I started thinking how hard it would be for him to do Trucking Tummy in the car. I imagined him having to stick his middle out so far that he'd be facing the roof instead of the windscreen. It was so silly that I giggled and he looked over at me, saying, "What's so funny?" But when I told him about it he shook his head and said, "Why's that such a big joke?"

I couldn't believe it. He always got my jokes in the truck. So I stopped cracking jokes, and I stopped telling him my ideas. I nearly stopped coming home from school too!

He didn't want to be a team. He didn't want to be anything.

Chapter Four

Chapter Four

....

I must have been looking as miserable as my
da, because one day my teacher handed me
a poster and said, "This might even cheer *you*
up, Kel Craven." At the time I thought
nothing could cheer me up, but I looked at
the poster anyway. It was about the District
Show and there was this big list of what was
on. Prize Bull competition, Prize Cake
competition (four categories), Prize this and
Prize that, but it was the small writing at the
bottom that caught my eye: Fathers' Nappy
Hanging Race.

I read it aloud, trying out the sound of it.
Malcolm Prentis heard me.

"My father always wins that," he said in a
very important voice.

"How much money does he get for it?" I
asked, thinking that Da might be able to earn

some from the race.

"Oh, duh, Craven," sneered Malcolm. "You don't win any *money*. You just do it. Dad's the best around."

Malcolm's words hit me like a slap in the face. That's exactly what they used to say about my dad when he drove his truck, that he was the best in the district.

The King … Number One.

As I sat there staring at the poster, an amazing feeling grew in my stomach. I was restless, I started to jiggle, then I wanted to run out of the building and scream. The best-ever idea of my whole life had just come to me.

My da could hang out nappies real fast. I'd watched him do it heaps of times. He could *win* that race.

OK, so it was only nappies and it wasn't truck driving, but once he'd had another taste of being Number One, he wouldn't be saying all that Mr Grump stuff like "I'm no good". And if my idea really worked, he might just

get back that other thing he left behind on
the truck with his red cap.

His smile.

Chapter Five

Chapter Five

....

Da was in the kitchen when I found him,
down on his knees picking up some broken
glass.

"Dad," I said, "I've got something to show
you."

"Not now, Kel," he growled. Then he
started muttering, "That little monster's got
a reach as long as a baboon's." He meant
Bridey, of course. She was standing in the
corner with a big grin on her face. I sat down
at the kitchen table as the little monster's
father poured the broken glass into the bin. A
good idea can always wait a little bit.

"It was one of your mother's best," said
Dad. He swept the last little bits of glass from
the floor, then went over to the stove, where a
big pot was boiling. Bridey had found an
interesting bit of fluff in the corner and she

was talking to it in her baby talk. Now was my chance. I pulled the scrunched up poster from my bag and held it out for Da to see.

"Have a look at this," I said.

He turned round, then grunted. "Don't know if we'll be able to afford many rides this year."

"It's not the rides I'm showing you," I said. I jabbed my finger at the writing near the bottom and he bent a bit closer to see what it said.

"Which one you pointing at? I can't tell."

"That one."

"Fathers' Nappy Hanging Race. What about it?"

Sometimes my dad can be very thick.

"You could win it with one hand tied behind your back, Da. I know you could."

"You have got to be joking," he snorted. "No way."

"Why not?" I asked.

"Because I'll look silly."

"But you won't. You're the best nappy

hanger in the district, no worries."

"That's exactly my point," he said.

Was it? What point?

Why wasn't he amazed by my idea? I thought he'd listen and say, "Now why didn't I think of that?" I thought he'd sit down with me to plan it out and I'd pull my chair in close to his, explaining how we could do it. And as I talked he'd have that same look on his face that he used to have on the truck, a sort of smile in his eyes. Then he'd say, "You're the ideas man, aren't ya, Kel?"

But he didn't.

Instead he took the poster and shoved it under a pile of old newspapers.

"Put your sister's shoes on," he bossed, with that tough look on his face again. "We're going into Dawson to do the shopping."

I grabbed Bridey's shoes and plonked her down on to the back porch. He didn't even care that I'd had the best idea of my life.

All he was worried about was looking silly.

Chapter Six

Chapter Six

On the way into Dawson I remembered something Da always said – "If the cap fits, wear it." He wasn't talking about his red KING cap, either. He explained it to me. If you're good at a job, then do it well, do it with pride. And he was good at hanging nappies. How could he look silly doing that? Especially if he won.

When we got to Dawson, Bridey started pointing at the rows of cans in the supermarket window. "My! My!" screamed Little Miss Extremely Destructive. Da was strapping her into the stroller when I said, "I'll take her for a walk if you like." He looked at me like he couldn't believe it. Most of the time I complain about having to look after my little sister, but this time was different. I was on a mission.

My mission took me to the Town Hall, where a big notice was pinned up: District Show Registration. It was where you came to register all your champion things for the competitions. Once I'd registered Da in the nappy race, and he had the official paper in his hand, he'd have to see that it wasn't silly. That it was a real race.

The lady at the desk looked up as I walked in. She smiled at Bridey, who was making a mess of an ice-cream I'd bought her to keep her quiet.

"You haven't come to register that delightful baby, have you?" she asked.

"No," I said. "I've come to register my dad."

"Register him in what, dear?" she asked.

"Fathers' Nappy Hanging Race," I announced, making it sound important.

The lady sort of half coughed, half choked, and looked down at the papers on her desk.

"We don't appear to have any registration forms for that one," she said. "Perhaps your father can just turn up on the day and enter."

"You sure?" I asked.

She nodded and smiled at me in that way that adults smile at very little kids. I smelt a rat. She thought hanging out nappies was silly too. But it was part of the District Show, wasn't it? And it was a lot more sensible than jumping around in a sack or holding an egg and spoon in your mouth.

I wheeled Bridey out of the Town Hall and leaned against the wall. Maybe this was a dumb idea. No one really thought much of nappies, especially not my da. I was about to give up when I heard a voice whining in my ear like a mosquito…

"Watcha doing?" It was Malcolm Prentis! "Did you bake a cake or something, Craven?"

"No," I said, trying to escape, but he had his father with him.

"Were you registering young Bridey in a baby competition?" asked Mr Prentis. That was the second time I'd heard that one, but I smiled politely and told him that I'd been asking about the nappy hanging race.

"My dad won that last year, did you know that?" asked Malcolm.

Of course I knew it. Malcolm had only mentioned it about two hundred thousand times.

"It's one of the highlights of the show," smiled Mr Prentis. "Now, don't tell me your father is going to enter this year."

"Maybe," I said.

"But that wouldn't be very fair, would it?" said Mr Prentis, sounding like he was shocked.

"What do you mean?" I asked.

"Well, the nappy race is for fathers who don't usually hang out nappies."

"Says who?" I said. I didn't like the way he was speaking.

"Says my dad," sneered Malcolm.

Great, both Prentises were ganging up on me.

"You see," said Mr Prentis, "your dad is getting a lot of practice with the nappies lately, from what I hear. So if he entered, it'd be like having one of the mothers in the competition."

"He's not one of the mothers," I yelled. "He's my da!"

"You're weird, Craven, you know that?" said Malcolm.

I didn't answer him, instead I rattled Bridey down the steps and walked away as fast as I could. My mind was steaming.

Oh sure, I'm weird because my da stays at home with a baby instead of working on a truck. Does that make James Cameron in year five weird too? Because his mum sells wooden toys and his dad hasn't got a job. And Sue Macclesfield doesn't even have a dad. Does Malcolm reckon she's weird as well?

Malcolm Prentis and his dad are the weird ones. Mr Prentis says nappies are women's work but he still likes to hang them out every year in the race. Come to think of it, the whole town of Dawson is weird. They put on a nappy hanging race and cheer their heads off at the nappy hangers, but if you try to talk to them about it they make out it's just a joke.

But I reckon deep down, people do take it seriously. People like Malcolm, who brags about his dad being the best nappy hanger in the district.

I wanted to run back to him and shout, "I'm gonna show you and your father and everyone else in this town that my da is still the best." Because if he wasn't the best, what was he? The King of the Grumps? And I know what that meant: "Kel, do this! Kel, do that! I don't have time to listen to any ideas!"

The trouble was, how was I going to get Mr Grump to enter this race? To make him see that "the cap fits"? It was then that I started imagining Da's reaction if I told him about what Mr Prentis had said. He'd be so mad. He might even yell, "I could beat that Mr Prentis any day!"

It was worth a try.

As soon as Bridey was strapped into the car and Mum was in the front seat, I told my champion nappy hanger about Mr Prentis. Then I waited. But he didn't say a word. He just gripped the wheel hard and stared at the road.

After a while, Mum spoke to him. "Does that make you feel mad, then?" she asked.

"No," he said quietly. "More embarrassed like."

"There's no shame in hanging out nappies," said Mum. "Personally, I've been doing it for years."

"I know," said Dad, scratching his head. "I'm just not one of them modern blokes. I don't mind doing it at home, but I'd feel like a goose hanging out nappies in front of the whole district."

"Why?" I asked from the back seat.

"Because fathers don't usually hang out nappies, do they?" he said. "I mean, that's why they have the race just for fathers. It's a joke."

Mum laughed. "I thought they had it for fathers because women were too sensible to be hanging out nappies when they didn't need to."

"But Mr Prentis doesn't think it's a joke," I said. "That's why he wins every year."

"Mate, I couldn't give a rat's tail about what Mark Prentis does," snorted Dad.

"Well, what about other fathers?" I shouted. "I bet you they hang out nappies like you. I bet all of them do it."

"I wouldn't count on it." Mum laughed.

I glared at Mum, giving her a *you're-supposed-to-be-on-my-side* look, but she just shrugged, then told Dad this long story about one of the girls at the supermarket. That was the end of that conversation.

I wasn't going to give up, no way. Slow and steady, that's how you get things done. My da had taught me that. Besides, another idea had skipped into my head.

It was the second best idea I'd ever had.

Chapter Seven

Chapter Seven

··

And what was my second best idea?
Research. The school had its "working bee"
that weekend. The place was crawling with
fathers who were hammering and sawing and
digging up things. It was the perfect
opportunity to ask them the one question my
da was too chicken to ask. "Do you hang out
nappies at home?" I had a piece of paper to
write down "yes" answers on the right, and
"no" answers on the left.

Some of the fathers laughed, or said they
did it years ago, and only once or twice. I put
them down as "no" because they didn't do it
all the time like my da. Six of them said "yes",
that they do hang out nappies, or that they
used to hang out nappies, and why was I
asking? That's when I told them about the
nappy hanging race and how they should

enter. When I'd finished my research I went and found Dad.

"Six," I announced grandly as my dad was filling a hole with cement.

He looked up at me and said, "What?"

"I found six fathers who hang out nappies."

"You still on about that?" he asked.

"Mr Daley, Mr Thing-a-me, you know, with the moustache?"

"Bandini."

"Yeah … and um … Mr Cheow, Mr Other-Thing-a-me and Mr O'Brien."

"O'Brien!" said my Da. "He hangs out nappies?"

"Yep." My da thinks Mr O'Brien is an important man because he owns a few shops or something.

"And they'll all be at the nappy hanging race, including Mr Prentis."

"Even though he thinks it's women's work," said Dad.

"Yeah, but it's not, is it? Fathers do hang out nappies. Now you can show all the other dads how good you are at it. And you don't need to look silly."

Dad just shook his head and said, "Amazing."

"So, what do you reckon?" I asked. "Will you do it?"

"I don't know," he said. "We'll talk about it later."

I nodded, trying to be very serious, but really I wanted to yell and skip. This was the first time he hadn't said "no" straight out.

The next day after school I ran all the way home from the bus stop. My legs were on fire. Now we could get the team started again, just like the old days. I found Da in the laundry with a basket full of clean clothes and nappies. Perfect!

"I see you're ready for a nappy training session," I said.

He laughed. "I thought you might have given up by now."

Given up? There was no way I'd give up. He shuffled up to the clothes-line, perching the basket on his fat tummy.

"It will be so easy, Da," I said as I caught up with him. "We'll practise every day."

"Well," he said as he plonked the basket on to the ground, "have you given any thought to what nappy hanging method I'll use, Coach?"

That stopped me cold. I'd never thought about what method he'd use, I'd only thought of him winning.

"You just hang nappies with pegs, don't you?" I shrugged.

He threw a nappy and two pegs at me, then asked me to show him how I would hang it.

"Because that's the sort of thing a coach does," he said.

I hung the nappy on the line, then I grabbed a few more. It was easy to hang nappies – why did he need a method? It wasn't complicated like driving a truck. In fact, the whole race was easy. Each father got twenty nappies, and the first father to hang out all his nappies won.

I grabbed some more nappies and pegged them quickly. OK, so he wanted a method, then that's what we'd do. The old team, heads together, working out the best way. Him saying, "Gee, I never thought of that before," and me looking serious and nodding. Then at the end, when the race was over, him grinning from ear to ear, shaking my hand saying, "I couldn't have done it without you, mate." I could see it so clearly.

But then I looked down at the basket and all I could see was clothes. There were no nappies left, I'd hung them all out. There was no sign of the nappy-hanger's father, either.

"Hey!" I shouted, when I spotted him in the sandpit with Bridey. "That's not fair. I'm not supposed to hang out the nappies, you are!"

"Well, you looked so happy doing them." He laughed again.

I marched over to the sandpit, where he was grinning like it was a huge joke. "You're not even taking this seriously," I said.

"Like Mr Prentis, you mean?" he asked.

"At least he wins something."

"It's just a nappy hanging contest, Kel."

"It's not!" I yelled. "It's a race. One you can win. Don't you get it? How else are you going to show people that you're still the best in the district? Don't you care about that any more? Don't you care about *anything*? Or did you leave your brain behind in the truck, too?"

"Hey, watch it," he said, looking mad.

"No, I won't," I said. I was just as mad as he was. "You think everything I say is silly now!" I sat down in the sandpit with my back to him, digging a deep hole to nowhere.

"Kel," he said, trying to cheer me up. "Come on, mate."

But I ignored him and after a while he sighed, then got up to hang out the rest of the washing. Bridey started dropping all her toys into my hole. Then she bent over and grabbed my face with her sandy hands, looking me in the eye as she made a very important point.

I cracked up, there's no way I can resist

Little Miss Extremely Cute. I gave her a kiss on the cheek and she rubbed it off, leaving a sandy streak across her face. Then I heard the flip-flop of Dad's thongs as he walked back to the laundry, and I felt bad again.

He used to play tricks on me when we were driving the truck. Funny tricks that made me laugh in the end. But getting me to hang out all the nappies wasn't funny, it was dumb. Why couldn't we do things together any more?

Bridey hopped into my lap and started hiding toys under my T-shirt. A rank smell wafted from her nappy, smothering me in a cloud of pong. Gross! My shorts were wet and my eyes were stinging.

I know my mum calls me melodramatic. I know she says I go on a bit, but this definitely was the worst afternoon of my life.

Chapter Eight

Chapter Eight

Later that night I was lying on my bed
thinking about the old days on the truck. The
long run when I was the Professor and Da
was Mr All-Night-Long. We knew every bit
of that road. The dangerous bends, the
straight parts where Da could play Trucking
Tummy, the good cafés and the terrible ones.
It was our highway.

What did we have now? Dirty dishes, bossy
orders and grumpy arguments.

My bedroom door opened and Da came in.
If he reckoned he was going to have one of
those father and son chats you see on TV,
then fat chance!

"Hey, Kel," he said, sitting on the edge of
my bed, "you talking to me yet?"

"What's the point?" I asked. "You wouldn't
listen to me anyway."

"You reckon?" he asked.

I didn't answer.

"Remember that drawing you did for me? The design for a hydraulic lift to empty out the trailer on the truck? I still got that, you know. It's real clever."

I sniffed, so what if he thought that was clever? It didn't mean anything now.

"Kel, mate. You're the ideas man, but some of your ideas ... well, they're a bit hard for an old coot like me to follow."

"Why?" I asked.

"I dunno, it's just the way I was made. I find it hard to get enthusiastic about housework ... maybe because I miss the truck so much."

"I miss it too. Why can't we get another one? Mum's working."

"Mate, I wish it was that simple. Nothing much is simple, really. I guess we just gotta live with what we got for now. But it don't mean we have to be miserable about it."

What did he mean, "*we*"?

"Anyway," he said, "I done some thinking. And I've come to a decision. You wanna know what it is?"

"Maybe," I shrugged.

"OK. Come with me," he said. "I got something to show you."

He took me outside to the clothes-line and pointed. "See that?" he said. All I could see were rows of white nappies in the moonlight.

"What about it?" I asked. Then I noticed something different. All the nappies I'd hung out had been moved to the front of the line.

"I been practising," said Dad. "Got it down to about two minutes."

"Hanging nappies?" I asked.

"Yep, twenty nappies, just like in the rules of the race. The first time it took me two minutes and forty-five seconds. That was a pretty crook time. I knew I could do better so I worked on me method, tried out a couple of ideas and kept beating me own record."

"Do you really mean it?" I asked. I had to make sure.

"Yep. You got me thinking, this afternoon. I been acting like a headless chook about this nappy business. Who gives a dog's scratch what the district thinks? You and Mum and Little Miss Extreme are the only ones that matter. Besides, I can't wait to see the look on Mark Prentis's face when I beat him."

I gave him a high-five and shouted "Yes!"

The team was back in action.

Chapter Nine

Chapter Nine

....

We practised every day after that. Da
perfected a method which he called "Gob,
Grab and Go". He'd put as many pegs into
his gob that would fit, then grab a handful of
nappies and go for it. We got our time down
to just under two minutes; then one minute
and fifty-three seconds; then an amazing one
minute and forty-two seconds which was the
record. If he went that fast in the nappy race,
no one could beat him.

And Dad's training got him thinking about
new methods he could try out for the
housework too. Like the "Sort and Box"
method for the clean clothes from the
clothes-line. He just sorted them out into
piles and chucked them into big boxes that
had our names on the side in crayon. I just
left my box by my bedroom door, which

meant I didn't have to put my clothes into drawers any more. Mum didn't think much of "Sort and Box".

"It's the dopiest idea I've ever encountered," she said, but in the end she agreed it was up to Da. "You're running the household now." You should have seen the grin on Da's face when she said that!

In between hanging nappies and doing housework, Da and me would sit together and he'd tell me stories. He told me about when I was two, a little bit older than Bridey. He used to drive up and down our road in the truck with me on his lap, and I'd laugh and jump up and down. He told me about driving in the early morning, with me still asleep in the cab behind him. About the mist coming up off the paddocks like the ground was melting in the sun. About the smell of the air at night, so salty and strong. I remembered that smell, how hungry it used to make me feel. Da sighed when he talked about those days.

"Things never turn out the way you plan 'em," he said.

Maybe that was true, but sitting with him like that, I didn't miss the truck so badly. Not with the nappies flapping in the wind behind us, the nappies he'd hung out with me timing him. Not with him asking me things like, "How did I go, Coach?" Then grinning at me the same way he used to grin in the truck.

The last day before the District Show we didn't bother with a training session. We just sat under the shady tree watching Bridey draw in the dirt.

"Do you ever wish you still had your red KING cap?" I asked him.

"It was just a hat," he said.

"But you wore it all the time."

"Yeah," he said, scratching his hair. "I suppose I did. I had that cap from when I started out driving. I was just a young buck then, come up from me parents' farm lookin' for work. That's when I met your mum, at a dance. I danced with her a couple of times, then I had the misfortune of having a bit of fun about her Irish accent."

I laughed. "She kicked you, right?"

"Dead on the shin. Had a bruise for ages. That's when I knew I loved her."

I groaned and grabbed him in a headlock and rolled him in the dirt. He needed a distraction from all this lovey-dovey stuff. We wrestled on the ground, with Bridey jumping up and down on us, until it was time to pick up Mum.

That night we ate fish and chips in Dawson, but Bridey was grizzly. Mum said it might be her teeth that were bothering her. We went home early, but I didn't mind. We needed our sleep because the next day was going to be huge.

Chapter Ten

Chapter Ten

....

What is it about teeth? Why couldn't we be
born with all of our teeth in our mouth and
not have to bother about them growing out
through little kids' gums?

I'd gone to bed that night a little nervous,
but I was tired enough to fall asleep easily.
The trouble was, my sleep didn't last very
long. And neither did Mum's or Dad's. I
woke up in the dark to the sound of Bridey
wailing. Our house is small and Bridey was
loud, so I couldn't get back to sleep.

On my way to the toilet I passed Mum in
the kitchen. She was searching through the
medicine cupboard, saying, "I don't believe
it!" over and over.

"What, Mum?" I asked.

She pointed to the cupboard, "There's no
painkiller left for the little one."

They'd forgotten to buy more.

I tried to get back to sleep, but Bridey was howling so loud that the walls started shaking, no kidding. Added to that was the sound of Dad rattling through the other cupboards looking for painkiller. And the sound of Mum shouting "Try the bathroom!" And the sound of Dad walking the little terror up and down the hallway trying to get her distracted by the patterns on the wallpaper. "See the pretty rose? Look, it's so red…"

In the end it all sort of blended into a long dream about me in a room full of crying babies, trying to take their nappies off so we could use them in the race.

It was a weird breakfast the next morning. There was Mum and me, sagging in our chairs with our tired eyes so red, Da over by the stove making eggs and bacon with the "Crack, Drop and Plop" method, looking like he'd fall asleep standing there. And next to us was Little Miss Extremely Happy, chirping away as cheerful as ever like nothing had happened. But then she dropped her breakfast on to the floor, and the whining started. It grew louder and louder, and nothing we could do would put her right. Mum sort of slumped down on to the kitchen table and groaned.

Da grabbed the keys and raced into Dawson for the painkiller. The Little Tooth Monster was crying at full speed by the time he returned with the bottle of pink liquid.

It worked like magic. She went to sleep on the big bed in Mum's arms, and Dad lay down too. I hopped into the middle and before long we were all asleep again, dreaming of nothing but peace and quiet.

I felt good when I woke up, my eyes were clear and my head felt light again. Then I looked at the clock. It was 1:30 pm, the District Show was half over and we had just over an hour until the nappy hanging race. We'd almost slept through it!

I shook Dad and Mum shouting, "Wake

up! Wake up! Get dressed!"

They were so sleepy that it took them for ever to get ready.

"Come on," I said, sounding just like them on a school morning. "We're late!"

I finally got them out the front door and into the car, and that was when the truck pulled up at our gate. Dad hopped out slowly to see what the driver wanted and I groaned. We'd never get to the race on time.

Chapter Eleven

Chapter Eleven

....

The driver came from a town that wasn't too far away. His name was Max, and he said he knew a bloke who knew a bloke who'd bought this second-hand truck and found a hat inside it. He said the address was written on the hat.

I shuffled from foot to foot. Why couldn't they all just hurry up and get on with it?

"So this bloke I know," drawled Max, "he reckons he knows the fella who owns the hat."

"Yes?" said Dad. He was so polite, I wanted to scream.

"So … this yours then?" asked Max. And he pulled out Dad's red KING cap from his back pocket.

Da couldn't believe it, he was grinning from ear to ear, saying it was amazing.

"This is very kind of you," said Mum, and Max went all red and said it wasn't far off his run. Then he went on to say that the fella he knew, who knew Dad, reckoned it would be a good idea to drop off the hat because Da always wore it.

Dad grinned again and asked Max if he wanted to come in and have a cup of tea. I glared at my father with a *what-about-the-race?* look, but he was too busy being happy because he'd got his red KING cap back.

So there we all stood, grinning and feeling pleased with ourselves, but not moving a muscle. Max said he'd better get back on the road, and I sighed with relief. But he still didn't go.

Then Max said that he knew of some work driving a truck if Da was interested. Mum stopped grinning then, and Dad scratched his head under the cap, saying he'd give it some thought.

Finally Max got back into his truck and waved goodbye and we piled into the car, heading for the District Show. As we drove towards town I looked at Dad wearing his red KING cap again. It was like he'd never lost it. I just knew he'd win the race now. Soon he would start driving again and everything would be how it was before. It was perfect.

"Hey, Da!" I shouted. "Isn't that brilliant about that truck-driving job?"

He didn't answer. Mum sighed and looked out the window and Da gave her quick little glances, but nobody spoke. It was very strange.

Then Mum sat up quickly and shouted, "Oh, no!" over and over, with me and Dad saying, "What?"

"How could I forget?" she shouted.

"Forget what?" asked Dad.

"The tennis club stall. I promised to help out this morning."

"Is that all," sighed Da.

"It's not your fault, Mum," I said. "Bridey was sick."

"Oh, but it was that snooty Jenny Cleave

who I was meant to be helping, and now she'll be going around saying I'm unreliable. It's taken me a long time to break into that club, I can tell you. I'll have to help out when we get there to make up for it."

"But what about Bridey?" I asked. "Who's going to look after her during the race?"

"Oh, she'll be all right," said Mum, in her airy-fairy voice. Then she added softly, to no one in particular, "I don't even like tennis."

Sure, Bridey would be all right, she always was. But what about us? What about Dad? What if the little terror decided to chuck another wobbly?

When we got to the show Mum ran to the tennis club stall apologizing all the way. Dad said we might as well have a look round so we took Bridey in her stroller and checked out the rides. The best by far was a spinning chair ride that went about a million kilometres per hour, but of course Little Miss NOW wanted a ride on the merry-go-round. We had just managed to get her off when they announced the Fathers' Nappy Hanging Race.

There were two long clothes-lines set up, with baskets of nappies arranged underneath and a huge pile of pegs in each basket. A crowd gathered as Da took up a spot closest to the front. Mr Prentis stood at the basket next to Dad, then along came Mr Cheow and Mr Bandini. Finally Mr O'Brien arrived and there was a big cheer from the crowd.

"All righty," said the show announcer. "This is the race you've been waiting for. Now we're going to see some real men in action. They have to hang out twenty nappies folks, corner to corner. And fellas, those are the nappies in the basket … the white things."

The crowd laughed at his silly joke and I could see Da sort of closing his eyes.

"Come on, Da!" I yelled to him, just in case he was losing his nerve.

He waved to me and the show announcer called out, "That's Danny Craven in the middle, folks. I hear the smart money is on him today."

Mr Prentis called out something, but it was drowned by the announcer shouting into the microphone. "Ready?! Ten, nine, eight, seven, six..." The crowd joined in, and the counting was so loud they must have heard it in the next district.

"... five, four, three, two, one!"

There was a loud bang and the race began. This was it, this was Da's big moment.

Chapter Twelve

Chapter Twelve

···

Dad was awesome. Not even Mr Prentis, with all his bragging, could keep up with him. The "Gob, Grab and Go" method was killing them. All the other fathers were still struggling with their third nappy by the time Da had hung out six. I stood at the front of the crowd cheering, forgetting all about being a coach.

Then I noticed that there was no sign of Bridey. In all the excitement I'd lost sight of her. It wasn't fair; why did she have to ruin everything? I called out for her, but there was no way she could hear me above all the cheering and laughing. I tried to push my way back through the crowd to find her, but I couldn't get through.

Then Malcolm Prentis stuck his face into mine and pointed towards the race. "Looks like your old man's got an extra nappy to hang out."

I turned around to see that Bridey was standing on tip-toes beside Da, begging him to pick her up. She was getting more and more upset, her voice rising to a scream. I went out to get her but she ran around Da's legs, playing a sort of screaming cat and mouse game with me. What did she think she was doing? There was a race going on.

It was so distracting that Dad had no choice but to pick her up and perch her on his hip. This left him with a big problem. How was he going to "Gob, Grab and Go" holding Bridey?

But my da is brilliant when it comes to making up clever methods. He plonked all his remaining nappies on top of his big, beanbag tummy. This left him with one hand holding Bridey and one hand free to peg nappies. I suppose he was now doing "Gut, Gob and Go". Whatever the name, it was working. Da could continue with the race, but he was slower. Mr Prentis had caught up already and Mr O'Brien wasn't too far behind.

Some of the people in the crowd were saying how cute Bridey looked, perched on Da's hip. *Cute!* She was a little monster! I heard another voice say that Da looked like a natural out there. And that was right because I'd seen Dad hold Bridey in one hand and try to do a job with the other a thousand times before.

Malcolm Prentis yelled that Da was a "show off" and that was right too. He was showing the whole district that he was the best dad around. And in a way I hadn't even planned.

But what about being the best nappy hanger? I realized with a shock that he was starting to fall behind. Holding Bridey was slowing him down heaps. He might still be able to win … it was going to be very close.

But then, a truly terrible thing happened.

Chapter Thirteen

Chapter Thirteen

Little Miss Ruin Everything started pulling the pegs from Da's mouth, one by one, and throwing them on to the ground. He was running out of them, and he tried shouting, "Thtopp Itthh!" but she wouldn't stop. So Dad put her down again and I ran up to grab her and she screamed louder than the entire crowd at the showground. Da had to pick her up on to his hip again to continue, but he'd lost even more time.

He was two nappies behind Mr Prentis by now. Da's one hand flew, banging the pegs in as fast as he could, the sweat trickling down from his KING cap.

The crowd got right behind him. I could hear people shouting, "Go, Danny!" and "Craven! Craven!" He flew past Mr O'Brien, but he was still one nappy behind Mr Prentis.

And no matter how hard he tried, he couldn't catch up. There were only four nappies left to hang. Unless something happened quick, Dad was going to be beaten by the boasting, bragging Mr Prentis. Then, in the middle of all the shouting and cheering and laughing, I heard music.

"Come on, little one," said my mother's voice. "Your da's got some work to do."

Mum must have heard all the shouting for "Craven" because she was standing there next to us with her arms out and the little screamer leapt right over to her.

Now Dad had two hands to work with, and you should have see him go. He was like a blur, nappies and pegs flying everywhere. Mr Prentis glanced over with a worried look on his face as Da quickly caught up.

Mum shouted, "Go, Danny," along with the rest of the crowd.

I was screaming, "Go-go-go!" and Bridey was just screaming.

Both men reached for their last nappy at

the same time, the sweat pouring from their heads, the crowd cheering so loud that the birds were in danger of dropping out of the sky. Both men placed their last nappy on the line and put the first peg in at the same moment. Then Mr Prentis had to bend for his second peg and Da simply pulled his from his mouth. This was it, my dad was going to win by a peg. But then something very weird happened – Da dropped his last peg. He'd never done that in any of our training sessions. It must have been the nerves or the pressure of the situation. By the time he'd pulled another from his mouth, Mr Prentis was putting his last peg on.

When I think about it now, I can see that final moment in slow motion, like the cricket replays. Mr Prentis pushing his peg on to the last corner of the last nappy. Da pushing his peg on a moment later, but being a lot quicker about it. Then the two of them removing their hands at the same moment and the crowd going berserk! Everyone was cheering and clapping but all Mr Prentis and my da could do was stand there panting, wondering who had won.

Finally the show announcer came on and said, "This is history in the making, folks. We have a dead heat!"

They'd *both* won!

The judge came out with the ribbons then, and you should have seen the look on my da's face when they pinned the ribbon on to his chest. He was grinning from ear to ear and I heard Mum say he looked "as proud as punch".

Mr Prentis shook Da's hand and told him it was a "manly effort" and Da smiled, saying "What else would you expect?" Then he put his arm around Mr Prentis and said, "You know, Mark, for a man who calls nappy hanging women's work, you're not bad at it. You don't hang nappies in secret, do you?" And Mr Prentis blushed as red as my dad's KING cap, then he laughed.

So there they were, the two kings of the nappies, and I reckon one of them was the best around.

Chapter Fourteen

Chapter Fourteen

....

We all relaxed after that, and I finally had a go on the spinning chair ride. In fact, I had three goes and would have had more but Mum said I'd lost the colour in my face and I had to sit down.

We ate ice-creams under a shady tree, me lying back on Mum's lap and Bridey climbing all over us. She knocked Da's KING cap off, and I picked it up. Then I remembered about the truck-driving job, and how no one had answered me the last time I asked about it.

"You *are* going to take that job on the truck, aren't you, Da?" I asked.

Mum and Da both went quiet again.

"Well, aren't you?" I repeated.

"It's not that simple," said Da.

"Why?" I asked.

"Well, it'd only be a short job," said Da.

"And you wouldn't be able to come with me…"

"Why not?"

"You wouldn't be covered by insurance. There'd be a company rule about it. Mate, it's not much fun driving for someone else. Besides, what about your mum? She likes her job … and staying home's not too bad for me."

"Not too bad!" Mum laughed. "Don't strain yourself, will you." Then she started pinching him on the arm.

"Ouch! Stop it! OK! OK! I *like* being at home. I get to discuss the world with my mate, Kel…"

"Bi-dee?" said Bridey, grabbing Da with her sticky hands.

"And I see more of Little Miss Sticky," grinned Dad.

"But what about the team?" I said, sitting up. "Aren't we ever going to get back on a truck again?"

"Of course we will," said Da. "But when the time's right."

My mum ran her fingers through my hair, the way I like it, then put her other hand on Da.

"Hey, Kel," she said, "*this* team is working fine. You, Da, me and the little one. In fact, I'd say we're in champion condition."

"Champion?" I asked.

"That's right," said Mum. "We've one champion worker…"

"Now who might that be?" joked Dad.

"Me, of course," grinned Mum. "We've one champion sticky fingers…"

"Little Miss Extreme," I laughed, rubbing her hair.

"And … we've one champion kid," smiled Mum, pointing at me.

"What about Da?" I said. "He's a champion nappy hanger now. It's official."

"Equal champion," shrugged Da.

"Amongst the men only," added Mum.

Dad grabbed Mum in a horse-bite on her knee, and she jumped so high that she lost her ice-cream. She gave him a pinch back and they had a play wrestle. Bridey crawled on to my lap and we watched.

So my best-ever idea ended up a bit differently, thanks to Bridey. Da said most things never turn out the way you plan them, but he wasn't exactly right. Because there he was with his big-kid grin and his red KING cap.

I reckon the old dad was finally back … just like I'd planned it.

PIMPLE-HEAD AND CURLY
by Ian Bone

Sometimes you have to dare to be different.

The River Gang girls have got it in for Rosie. They used to be her friends, but now they call her Pimple-head. They make fun of her dog, too. Worst of all, they've turned the new girl, Curly, against her. Is she brave enough to risk being laughed at and make a stand?

This is a warm, perceptive and inspiring story for young readers by the award-winning author of *Winning Back Dad*.